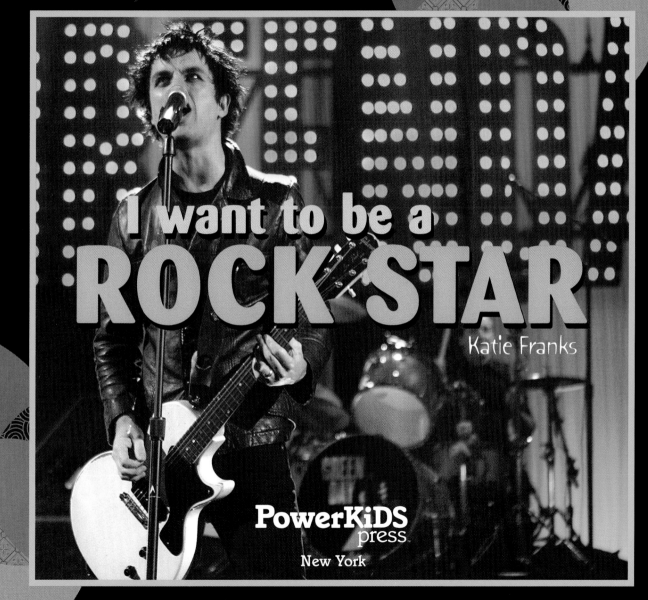

dream jobs™

I want to be a
ROCK STAR

Katie Franks

PowerKiDS
press.

New York

To my editor, who made me the best writer I could be

Published in 2007 by The Rosen Publishing Group, Inc.
29 East 21st Street, New York, NY 10010

First Edition

Editor: Jennifer Way
Book Design: Ginny Chu
Photo Researchers: Sam Cha and Ginny Chu

Photo Credits: All Photos © Getty Images.

Library of Congress Cataloging-in-Publication Data

Franks, Katie.
  I want to be a rock star / Katie Franks. — 1st ed.
     p. cm. — (Dream jobs)
  Includes index.
  ISBN-13: 978-1-4042-3618-9 (library binding)
  ISBN-10: 1-4042-3618-X (library binding)
  1. Rock music—Juvenile literature. 2. Rock musicians—Juvenile literature. I. Title.
  ML3534.F734 2007
  781.66—dc22
                                        2006019457

Manufactured in the United States of America

Contents

Beck is a rock star who has made many albums and appeared in many magazines.

A Fun Career

You have heard rock music on the radio. You have probably seen rock stars on television and in magazines. Maybe you have even been in the **audience** at a rock show. Maybe you dream of a **career** playing in a rock band. There are many interesting things rock stars get to do as part of their jobs. This book will show you some of the things rock stars do.

The Black Eyed Peas are (from left to right) will.i.am, Fergie, apl.de.ap, and Taboo. Here they are walking the red carpet at the 2006 Grammys.

Walking the Red Carpet

There are many **awards** given out to honor musicians each year. These awards include the Grammys, the Billboard Music Awards, and the American Music Awards. Each year there is a **ceremony** at which the awards are presented. You can usually find lots of pictures taken of rock stars as they are walking into the ceremony. This is known as walking the **red carpet**. Going to an award ceremony and walking the red carpet can be **exciting**.

Meg White plays the drums for the White Stripes. The White Stripes usually use only two instruments, guitar and drums.

Playing Instruments

When you listen to a rock band, you can hear several instruments being played. The most common instruments include guitars, bass guitars, drums, keyboards, and voices. Learning to play an instrument takes a lot of practice. The members of a band practice their instruments so that they can play them well. Bands also must practice playing together. Many bands also use this **rehearsal** time to write new songs.

This is the producer Nigel Godrich with Fran Healy of the band Travis. They are working at the mixing board in a recording studio.

Making Albums

When a rock band makes an album, they go to a recording **studio**. At the recording studio each person records his or her part of a song separately. These separate parts are called tracks. These tracks are then mixed together into the song you will hear on the album. To do this rock bands usually work with a **producer**. The machine a producer uses to mix songs is called a mixing board.

Bono, the lead singer of U2, is signing autographs for fans.

Meeting Fans

Rock stars have lots of fans who buy their records and go to their concerts. Rock stars also sometimes get to meet their fans in person. They might appear at an event at a record store at which they sign copies of their albums for their fans. Many fans like to collect the **autographs** of their favorite rock stars. It is fun for fans to have a chance to meet their favorite rock stars.

The Scottish band Franz Ferdinand has toured all around the world to play for their fans.

Touring the World

An important part of a rock star's career is playing concerts. Concerts can be held at small clubs, theaters, or **arenas**. Rock bands usually go on tour and play a lot of concerts. A rock band on tour may travel by airplane or on a special tour bus. When a band goes on tour, they travel from city to city to put on concerts. Some rock bands even get to tour the whole world!

Audiences enjoy seeing their favorite rock stars in concert.

Playing Concerts

Concerts are as exciting for rock stars as they are for their fans. Can you imagine being a rock star on stage and playing in front of thousands of people? Being in the audience at a rock show is fun, too. Fans enjoy dancing to the music and seeing their favorite band play live. Sometimes to make the concert special, the band will show **videos**, or have special lighting.

Clay Aiken (left) and Ruben Studdard (right) helped present Kelly Clarkson with a platinum record in 2003.

Going Platinum

Rock stars receive special awards for selling lots of records. These awards are called gold records and platinum records. In the United States, a gold album is given for selling 500,000 copies of a record. Platinum records are given for one million copies of a record sold. When a rock star receives a gold record or a platinum record, he or she is presented with a special copy of the album.

In 2006, Missy Elliot won her sixth Grammy. Here she is with the Grammy she won in 2004.

Winning Grammys

The Grammy Awards are held each year. Music fans can watch the Grammys on television to see if their favorite rock stars win an award. A Grammy is one of the biggest awards a rock star can win. The Grammys recognize outstanding **achievements** in music. The winners are chosen by people who work in the music business. When rock stars win Grammys, they can feel proud that their peers think their music is well done.

The Hall of Fame

One of the highest honors for a rock star is to be **inducted** into the Rock and Roll Hall of Fame. Each year a small group of rock stars is chosen for this honor. A rock star can be inducted into the hall of fame 25 years after the **release** of his or her first record. The Rock and Roll Hall of Fame Museum is in Cleveland, Ohio.

Glossary

achievements (uh-CHEEV-mints) Accomplishments.

arenas (uh-REE-nuhz) Fenced or walled-in spaces that are used for events.

audience (AH-dee-ints) A group of people who watch or listen to something.

autographs (AH-toh-grafs) A person's name, written by that person.

awards (uh-WORDZ) Things that are given to someone as a prize.

career (kuh-REER) Job.

ceremony (SER-ih-moh-nee) A special series of actions done on certain occasions.

exciting (ik-SY-ting) Very interesting.

inducted (in-DUKT-id) To have been made a member.

producer (pruh-DOO-ser) A person who makes records.

red carpet (RED KAR-pet) The walkway that leads to the building where an event is being held. This walkway is usually covered with a red carpet.

rehearsal (rih-HER-sul) At time during which someone practices something, such as music.

release (ree-LEES) The putting out of something.

studio (STOO-dee-oh) A room or building where an artist works.

videos (vih-DEE-ohz) Short films.

Index

Web Sites

Due to the changing nature of Internet links, PowerKids Press has developed an online list of Web sites related to the subject of this book. This site is updated regularly. Please use this link to access the list: www.powerkidslinks.com/djobs/rock/